EFTA European Free Trade Area

EHF extremely high frequency

ENT ear, nose and throat

ESN educationally sub-normal

ESP extra-sensory perception

ETA estimated time of arrival

ETD estimated time of departure

FA Football Association

FBI Federal Bureau of Investigation (USA)

FC Football Club

FO Foreign Office

Fr. Father; Friar; France

GB Great Britain

GBH grievous bodily harm

GCE General Certificate of Education

GDR German Democratic Republic (East Germany)

GLC Greater London Council

GMT Greenwich Mean Time

GP general practitioner (doctor)

GPO General Post Office (now PO)

HB hard black (pencil lead)

HGV heavy goods vehicle

HM Hea... Hea...

HM Ins...

HM Maj... Ship

HMSO His/Her Majesty's Stationery Office

HRH His/Her Royal Highness

IBA Independent Broadcasting Authority (formerly ITA)

ICI Imperial Chemical Industries

ILEA Inner London Education Authority

IMF International Monetary Fund

IOU I owe you (written promise to pay)

IQ intelligence quotient

IRA Irish Republican Army

ITA Independent Television Authority (now IBA)

JP Justice of the Peace

Jr junior

K2 2nd highest mountain in world, in India 8610m

KGB Komitet Gosudarstvennoi Bezopasnosti – Russian secret police

LEA Local education authority

LP long playing record; Lord Provost; low pressure

...i, ...K

...rts

...f the ...sh Empire

MC Master of Ceremonies

MD Managing Director; Medical Dept; Doctor of Medicine

MI Military Intelligence

MI5 Military Intelligence section 5

MI6 Military Intelligence section 6

MOD Ministry of Defence

MOT Ministry of Transport

NAAFI Navy, Army & Air Force Institutes

NALGO National Association of Local Government Officers

NASA National Aeronautics and Space Administration (USA)

NATO North Atlantic Treaty Organisation

NATSOPA National Society of Operative Printers, Graphical and Media Personnel

NB nota bene – Latin for note well

NCB National Coal Board

NCCL National Council for Civil Liberties

Abbreviations continued on inside back cover

*This will be a useful reference book for the whole family.
It is packed with fascinating information about the English
language.*

Contents

Acknowledgment:
The compiler and publishers would like to thank
Andrew M Hunt BA (Hons) Dip Ed for his help during the
preparation of this book.

First Edition

© LADYBIRD BOOKS LTD MCMLXXXIV

the Ladybird book of SPELLING and GRAMMAR

compiled by DOROTHY PAULL
designed and illustrated
by JOHN BRADFORD of
HURLSTON DESIGN LTD

Ladybird Books Loughborough

The alphabet

The word is formed from two words: *alpha* and *beta*, which are the first two letters of the Greek alphabet.

The English language has developed very gradually from several more ancient languages. Our present day alphabet of twenty six letters forms the basis of the language.

Two sentences often used to train typists contain all twenty six letters:
> *Whenever the black fox jumped, the squirrel gazed very suspiciously.*
> *The quick brown fox jumps over the lazy dog.*

The alphabet consists of five *vowels* – **a e i o u**
and twenty one *consonants* **b c d f g h j k l m n p q r s t v w x y z.**
The word VOWEL comes from the Latin word
VOWIS meaning *voice*.
CONSONANT comes from the Latin word
CONSONARE meaning *to sound together*.

Most words contain some vowels and there are a few which contain all five vowels:
> *facetious   abstemious   tambourine*

A few words do not have any vowels at all but they usually have the letter **y** instead, used in a way which sounds like a vowel.
> *hymn   why   lynch*

CAPITALS or UPPER CASE LETTERS
ABCDEFGHIJKLMNOPQRSTUVWXYZ
LOWER CASE LETTERS
abcdefghijklmnopqrstuvwxyz

The upper and lower cases were the cases in which printers kept their metal type.

The arrangement of the letters is based on frequency of use rather than alphabetical order. The most-used letter is **e**.

4

The style of alphabet we use is the Roman alphabet. It developed over thousands of years through Egyptian, Phoenician and Greek alphabets.

Egyptian	Phoenician	Greek	Roman

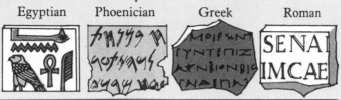

Alphabetical Order

Reference books, directories, dictionaries and filing systems all use the alphabet as a means of ordering information.

In the UK letters are used together with numbers on car registration plates. These plates give specific information.

the number of cars using GB in the year A –

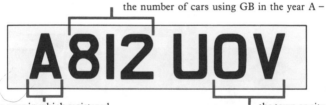

the year in which registered
from August 1st (83-84)

the town or city
in which registered

Before August 1983 when the new sequence was introduced, a similar system was used but the year letter was at the end eg ASD 498 Y

The USA has no national system. Each state has its own method of registration.

Postcodes also contain letters and numbers in the UK. Using the postcode the Post Office sorting office can sort letters very quickly by machine.

small section of area

main city or town
in postal area

CV 13 OLZ

the street or
part of a street

In the USA zip codes use numbers only to indicate the town or city. No other information is contained in them eg 80302 Boulder, Colorado.

A Sentence

A sentence consists of a group of words, one of which must be a VERB. The VERB is the action or doing word. The person or thing doing the action is the *subject* of the sentence. The subject is either a NOUN or a PRONOUN.

If the action is being done to someone or something, that is the *object* of the sentence, and is also a NOUN or a PRONOUN.

*The boy bounced the **ball**.*

Other groups of words also do specific jobs in a sentence. A word telling you more about the boy or the ball is an ADJECTIVE.

*The boy bounced a **blue** ball.*

When we introduce a word to tell us more about how he bounced the ball, we use an ADVERB.

*The big boy **lazily** bounced a blue ball.*

This sentence is more interesting because it tells us a lot more.

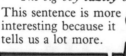

The words *the* and *a* are the ARTICLES: *the* is a particular or **definite** article and *a* (or *an*) is any article or the **indefinite** article. They have no meaning themselves but refer directly to the noun which always follows them.

*Give me **the** book from **the** shelf.*

***A** book makes **a** good present.*

An is used before a word that starts with a vowel, e g *an egg*. Some words starting with **h** also require *an* before them – *an heir, an hour*.

A sentence always starts with a capital letter and ends with a full stop ., a question mark ? or an exclamation mark !

If we make the sentences longer by adding more words, or a phrase or sentence, we need a CONJUNCTION *(see page 15)*.

*The big boy lazily bounced a blue ball **and** it rolled away from him.*

and is the CONJUNCTION which joins the two parts of a sentence together.

it is used instead of the ball and is a PRONOUN *(see page 14)*.

him is used instead of the boy and is also a PRONOUN.

} The pronoun replaces the noun.

away tells us more about the way the ball rolled, and is an ADVERB *(see page 22)*.

from is a PREPOSITION *(see page 15)* which is used before a noun or pronoun.

Words such as ***Ah! Oh! Eh!*** are INTERJECTIONS. These are the last group or family of words which are needed to complete the sentence structure.

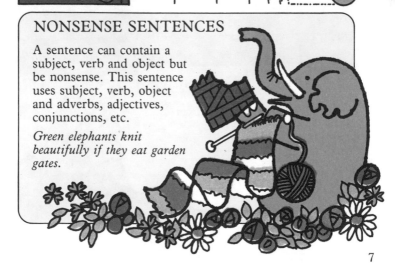

NONSENSE SENTENCES

A sentence can contain a subject, verb and object but be nonsense. This sentence uses subject, verb, object and adverbs, adjectives, conjunctions, etc.

Green elephants knit beautifully if they eat garden gates.

Nouns

A noun is a word which refers to a person, a place, a thing or a title. There are two groups: *common nouns* and *proper nouns*. Common nouns do not have capital letters (unless they begin a sentence). Proper nouns always start with a capital letter.

Common Nouns

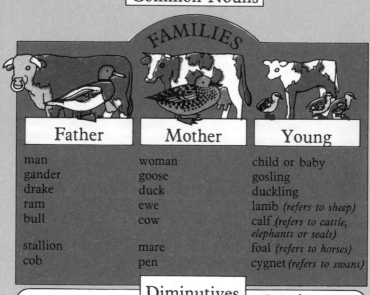

FAMILIES

Father	Mother	Young
man	woman	child or baby
gander	goose	gosling
drake	duck	duckling
ram	ewe	lamb *(refers to sheep)*
bull	cow	calf *(refers to cattle, elephants or seals)*
stallion	mare	foal *(refers to horses)*
cob	pen	cygnet *(refers to swans)*

Diminutives

A diminutive is a small version of something larger.

booklet from *book*
rivulet from *river*

Some nouns indicate size.

a speck
a splinter

Abstract nouns

These nouns are the names of things which cannot be seen or touched.

honesty
corruption
love
hope

Concrete nouns

These nouns are the names of things which can be seen and touched.

torch
car
book
apple

Homes

Examples:

Person	Home
archbishop	palace
monk	monastery
nun	convent
minister	manse
parson	parsonage
rector	rectory
vicar	vicarage

Creatures (wild)	Home	Domesticated or in captivity	
badger	sett	birds	aviary
fox	earth	bees	hive or
hare	form		apiary
otter	holt	dog	kennel
squirrel	drey	cow	byre or shed

Nouns continued

Gender denotes sex...masculine, feminine or neuter

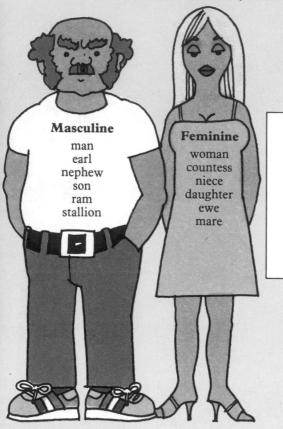

Masculine

man
earl
nephew
son
ram
stallion

Feminine

woman
countess
niece
daughter
ewe
mare

Common
can be either

person
baby
friend
owner
pupil
teacher
visitor

Neuter
is neither male nor female

apple   envelope   kettle
chimney   garage   umbrella

Some examples of other common nouns not requiring a capital letter.

Occupations	Places of Work	Containers	Noises
doctor	surgery	barrel	gibber
dentist		caddy	buzz
florist	flower shop	cruet	croak
mechanic	garage	envelope	squeal
teacher	school	punnet	groan

THE FIVE SENSES
used by humans and animals
to perceive the world.

THE FOUR ELEMENTS
thought by the ancient world
to make up the universe.

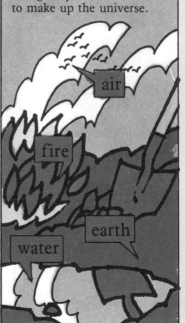

Collective nouns

Collective nouns indicate a group or collection of persons or things. A collective noun is usually singular *(see page 24)* and does not have a capital letter.

eg *A **swarm** of bees **is** in the apple tree.*

Exceptions

When the collective noun refers to something specific, it has capital letters but is still singular.

eg *the British Government, Parliament*

Animals

a flock of sheep
a litter of puppies
a covey of grouse
a clowder of cats
a school of whales
a siege of herons
a murder of crows
a dule of doves
a pride of lions
a leap of leopards
a parliament of owls
a crash of rhinoceroses
a swarm of bees
a cete of badgers

Objects

a bunch of grapes
a bouquet of flowers
a clutch of eggs
a bale of cotton
a fleet of ships, cars
a pack of cards
a flight of stairs
a batch of bread
a punnet of strawberries
a quiver of arrows

People

a board of directors
a host of angels
a bench of magistrates
a crowd of people
a congregation *(church)*
a commune *(a group living and working together)*

Proper nouns

These always have a capital letter.

Places

Australia	London
Barnsley	South America
Denmark	Wellington
Europe	New York

People

(real or fictitious)
Red Riding Hood
Sherlock Holmes
John Paul II
Daley Thompson
Julius Caesar
Gandhi

Titles

Star Wars

Hamlet

Paddington Bear

The Ascent of Man

13

Pronouns

A pronoun is used in place of a noun to avoid repetition.
There are three groups:

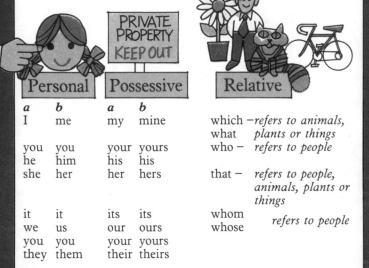

Personal		Possessive		Relative
a	*b*	*a*	*b*	
I	me	my	mine	which –*refers to animals,*
				what *plants or things*
you	you	your	yours	who – *refers to people*
he	him	his	his	
she	her	her	hers	that – *refers to people,*
				animals, plants or
				things
it	it	its	its	whom
we	us	our	ours	whose *refers to people*
you	you	your	yours	
they	them	their	theirs	

When the person is doing the action – the subject of the
sentence – use a pronoun from column *a*:
personal – ***You** and **I** will go together.*
possessive – column *a* plus the noun. ***Her** hair is very curly.*

When the action is being done to the person – the object of
the sentence – use a pronoun from column *b*:
personal – *The teacher shouted at **him** and **me**.*
possessive – instead of the noun use a word from column *b*.
*The book is **hers**.*

After a preposition (eg from, after – *see page 15*) always treat
the pronoun as the object of the sentence and use a word
from column *b*. *The dog chased after **him**.*

Relative pronouns refer back to an earlier noun or pronoun.
*Susan gave me a book **which** I had not read.*

A preposition is used before a noun or pronoun to indicate **place** (eg above, behind), **position** (eg on, among) or **time** (eg since, until).

Other examples of prepositions are:

into	across	against	at	through
over	under	past	between	with
by	within	beyond	after	beneath
upon	beside	off	into	underneath
overhead	around	along	towards	up

*The frog jumped **into** the pond and disappeared **beneath** the surface.*

Con **junctions**

Conjunctions join together two words, two phrases or two parts of a sentence:

or	if	and	but	because	that
for	before	since	yet	as	although
	while	unless	both		either/or
neither/nor	wherever		until	till	lest
even if	except that	so that			

eg *You **and** I are going into town today.*
*We cannot stay long **because** it is getting dark.*

15

Adjectives

An adjective is used to tell more about a noun or pronoun so that it adds something to the meaning. It used to be called an AD-NOUN but now it is often referred to as a describing word. An adjective usually comes immediately before the noun in a sentence. More than one adjective can be used with each noun or pronoun. When describing a pronoun it follows the verb.

eg *After falling in the muddy water, they were wet and hungry.*

Adjectives fall into three groups:

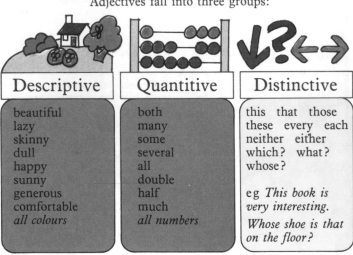

Descriptive	Quantitive	Distinctive
beautiful lazy skinny dull happy sunny generous comfortable *all colours*	both many some several all double half much *all numbers*	this that those these every each neither either which? what? whose? eg *This book is* *very interesting.* *Whose shoe is that* *on the floor?*

Descriptive adjectives are often formed from a noun:
good from *goodness*   *sunny* from *sun*
Others relating to animals are often formed from Latin words for that animal:
feline from *felis* for cat
bovine from *bovis* for bull
canine from *canis* for dog
leonine from *leo* for lion

The opposite page shows the positive forms of the adjective used when only one thing is being described.

When an adjective is used to compare two or more things, it changes form.

a The tall girl came into the room.
(one girl...use the **positive** form)

b This girl is taller than that one.
(two girls... use the **comparative** form)

c That girl is the tallest in the room.
(more than two girls...use the **superlative** form)

Positive	Comparative	Superlative
high	higher	highest
dull	duller	dullest
Exceptions:		
good	better	best
bad	worse	worst

When an adjective has two or more syllables, *more* and *most* are used with the positive form.

handsome	*more* handsome	*most* handsome
beautiful	*more* beautiful	*most* beautiful
unusual	*more* unusual	*most* unusual

e g *The most beautiful butterfly I have ever seen came into the garden today.*

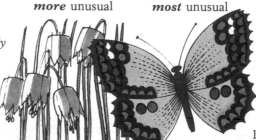

17

Verbs

A verb is the most important word in a sentence; it is the action or **doing** word.

Without it we are unable to make a sentence.

Examples:

You *read* this page. *Read* this page. *Read* this. (All sentences)

You this page (Not a sentence)

Read is the word which makes the difference. It is the VERB.

The person doing the action is the subject of the sentence. Sometimes the subject is doing something to someone or something. That is the object of the sentence.

Sometimes an auxiliary verb is used with a participle in the present and past tenses *(see page 21)*.

Some verbs always need an object to make sense. They are TRANSITIVE verbs. Verbs which do not need an object are INTRANSITIVE.

Transitive	Intransitive
need an object	*do not need an object*
to give	to speak
to do	to laugh
to expect	to ride
to make	to walk
to find	to listen
to catch	to cry
to ask	to roar

✓ Need an object

✗ Do not need an object

Verbs: tenses

To indicate *time* we change the form of the verb. These forms are the *tenses*; a word from the Latin word *tempus* meaning time.

Present tense

(is happening now)
I help
you help
she/he helps
you help (plural)
we help
they help

Past tense

(has happened)
I helped
you helped
she/he helped
you helped (plural)
we helped
they helped

Future tense

(will happen)
I shall help
you will help
she/he will help
you will help (plural)
we will help
they will help

Conditional tense

(may happen if…)
I would help
you would help
she/he would help
you would help (plural)
we would help
they would help

Participles: past and present

Participles are parts of verbs which are used with another verb in a sentence to change the tense. The other verbs called auxiliary (helping) verbs are *was* and *is*.

burnt – past participle
Joan of Arc **was** burnt at the stake.

burning – present participle
The fire **is** burning brightly.

Participles are also used as adjectives, to describe nouns etc.

*The **burnt** toast was inedible. John warmed his hands by the brightly **burning** fire.*

burnt and **burning** are used here as adjectives.

Present participles	Past participles
speaking	spoken
doing	done
playing	played
crying	cried
forgetting	forgotten
catching	caught

Auxiliary Verbs – tenses

Sometimes an auxiliary verb is used with a participle in the present and past tenses.

*I **am** helping*

*I **was** helped*
*I **had** helped*

Present tense
I *drive* to work every day.
I *am driving* today.

Future tense
I *shall cut* out my new dress tomorrow.
You *will get* your birthday cards in the morning.

Past tense
I *forgot* to take a coat.
I *have forgotten* to buy some bread.

Conditional tense
The school team *should* reach the final if it wins this round.
I *would* expect you to behave yourself if you went to the cinema.
I *would* have gone to the shops if they hadn't been closed.

Do not confuse

can and may

Can I do something? means, 'Am I physically able to do something?'
eg *Can I play football with a sore foot?*

May I do something? means, 'Will I be allowed to do it by someone else?'
eg *May I play football with you, please?*

Adverbs

An adverb tells more about a verb, an adjective or another adverb. The word adverb means *added word*. It is placed immediately before or after the word it is describing. There are three basic groups which tell **how**, **when** or **where** something happened.

Other adverbs tell how many times or how much something is done eg twice.

How		**When**	**Where**
These are formed by		soon	here
*adding **ly** to the adjective*		often	there
easily	softly	yesterday	everywhere
quickly	heavily	always	somewhere
noisily	eagerly	after	along
		seldom	beside

eg *Susie **easily** reached the final of the tennis tournament.*

*The plane will be taking off **soon**.*

*Boris is hiding **somewhere** upstairs.*

Adverbs, like adjectives, also have comparative and superlative forms. These are formed by using **more** and **most** or **less** and **least** with an adverb.

eg *The thrush moved **more quickly** than the snail.*

*The robin is one of the **most easily** recognised birds.*

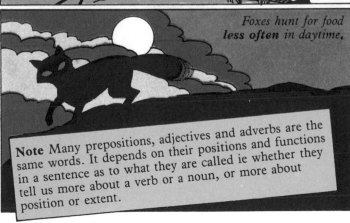

*Foxes hunt for food **less often** in daytime.*

Note Many prepositions, adjectives and adverbs are the same words. It depends on their positions and functions in a sentence as to what they are called ie whether they tell us more about a verb or a noun, or more about position or extent.

Singular and Plural

one thing is singular
more than one is plural

a Some nouns only require an *s* to form the plural:
cat/*cats* balloon/*balloons* dog/*dogs*

b Some nouns require *es* to form the plural:
fish/*fishes* potato/*potatoes* fox/*foxes* dress/*dresses*

c A few ending in *o* only require *s*:
photo/*photos* avocado/*avocados* solo/*solos*

d Those nouns ending in *y* following a consonant change
y to *i* and add *es*:
party/*parties* lady/*ladies* fly/*flies* city/*cities*

e Nouns ending in *y* following a vowel only add *s*:
day/*days* monkey/*monkeys*
valley/*valleys* boy/*boys*

f Some nouns ending in *f* change to *v*
and add *es*:
sheaf/*sheaves* loaf/*loaves* calf/*calves*

g Most nouns ending in *f* or *fe* simply
add *s*:
chief/*chiefs* roof/*roofs* giraffe/*giraffes*
Exceptions: wife/*wives* knife/*knives*
half/*halves*

h A few nouns have plurals which do not
fit into any of the above groups:
goose/*geese* child/*children* oasis/*oases*
foot/*feet* tooth/*teeth* mouse/*mice*
medium/*media*

j Some words keep the same form in the
plural:
salmon deer aircraft sheep trout

Noun and Verb Agreement

In a sentence the subject and verb must always be in agreement: a *singular noun* with a *singular verb* form, a *plural noun* with a *plural verb* form.

The ship sets sail today. *Singular*
The ships set sail tonight. *Plural*
He enjoys being at home. *Singular*
Many people enjoy going to a football match. *Plural*

Some nouns appear to be plural but are in fact singular:

mathematics physics news
eg *The news **is** very interesting today.*

Singular verbs are used with some phrases:

each of neither of either of everybody no one
eg *Everybody **will be** there.*

Collective nouns are the ones which usually cause problems.
The words are singular but their meanings are plural.
army class government team group school
The noun, verb and any pronoun must all be in agreement.
eg *All the **class is** coming to watch the play.*
*The **school is** on holiday so **its** rooms are empty.*

Apostrophes

The apostrophe ' is used for two very different purposes:

1 *to show something belongs to someone*

Singular
*a **boy's** shoes*
*an old **man's** beard*
*the **dog's** dinner*

Plural
*the **boys'** shoes*
*the old **men's** beards*
*the **dogs'** dinner*

THE APOSTROPHE COMES
BEFORE THE **s** IN THE
SINGULAR.
Exceptions: its ours
yours theirs hers his
e g *The cat opened its mouth.*

THE PLURAL HAS THE
APOSTROPHE AFTER THE
PLURAL FORM. ADD AN **s**
WHERE THE PLURAL DOES
NOT HAVE ONE.
e g *men   men's*

2 *to show that a letter or letters are missing from a word*
   I have...*I've*   who have...*who've*   it is...*it's*
   you will...*you'll*   you have...*you've*   cannot...*can't*
   does not...*doesn't*   do not...*don't*   will not...*won't*
   shall not...*shan't*   have not...*haven't*
   all is well...*all's well*   of the clock...*o'clock*
   there is...*there's*   is not...*isn't*   who would...*who'd*
   e g *I **can't** decide where to go.*
   ***Isn't** it cold today?*

26

Sentence Structure

Simple sentences

A simple sentence conveys one idea or thought and has one VERB:

> *Julian **has** a rabbit.*
> *Simon and Anna **are** on holiday.*

Complex sentences

A complex sentence conveys more than one idea or thought and has more than one VERB:

> *Julian **has** a rabbit which **has** black ears and **is** called Peter.*
> *Simon and Anna **are** going on holiday and they **will** go swimming in the sea.*

Two or more simple sentences can be put together using CONJUNCTIONS to form complex sentences:

> *Sarah and James ride their bicycles every day.*
> *They do not go out if it rains.*

can become

> *Sarah and James ride their bicycles every day **but** they do not go out if it rains.*

Complex sentences can be made into simple sentences:

> *Rachel found a brooch **which** was very valuable.*

can become

> *Rachel found a very valuable brooch.*

A SENTENCE ALWAYS STARTS WITH A CAPITAL LETTER AND ENDS WITH A FULL STOP, A QUESTION MARK OR AN EXCLAMATION MARK.

Spelling

Silent *e*

When a word ends in a silent *e* the earlier vowel says its *name* instead of its *sound*:
In *cape* the *a* is long...(compare this with *cap*)
  e g *code bite cute*

Adding an ending

a When adding *ing er able ious en ous y* to words ending in *e*, leave off the *e*:
   take/*taking* fame/*famous* write/*writing* believe/*believable*
   Exceptions: shoe/*shoeing* singe/*singeing*
                    agree/*agreeable* – *agreeing*

   Keep the e when adding endings beginning with a consonant: *ment worthy less ful*
   tasteless advancement hopeful praiseworthy

b When adding *full* to a word, drop the final *l*:
   beautiful careful

c For words ending in *ge*, keep the *e* when adding *able* or *ous*:
   manage/*manageable*

d For words ending in *ie*, change the *ie* to *y* and add *ing*:
   die/*dying* lie/*lying*

e For words of one or more syllables ending in a *y*, change *y* to *i* before adding *es er eth ly ness ed*:
   forty/*fortieth* busy/*busily* – *business*
   occupy/*occupied* early/*earlier* apology/*apologies*

f Words ending in *y* following a vowel, keep the *y* when adding the endings *er ing ed*:
   pray/*praying* – *prayer* – *prayed*
   fray/*fraying* – *frayed*
   say/*saying*

Rules

ie and ei

1 When *ie* and *ei* sound like *ee* in cheese, then *i* comes before *e* *except after* *c*:
   believe frieze receive retrieve conceit cashier
   Exceptions: weird seize weir

2 Sometimes *ei* says *i*:
   height neither eiderdown either sleight

3 *ei* and *ie* can sound like *e* as in egg:
   friend leisure

4 or like *ai* in rain: neighbour skein reign eight

5 or like *i* in give: sieve

Doubling Final Consonants

1 When a word of one syllable ends in a single consonant, following a single vowel – eg *run fun bat big mad wag* – double the consonant before adding *ed er est ing*:
   eg running funniest madden wagging biggest batter
   Words ending in *r*, *x*, *w* or *y* are exceptions to this rule.
   eg answer/*answered* box/*boxer*

2 When another consonant or a pair of vowels comes before the final consonant – eg be*l*t or ba*i*l – simply add the ending: belted bailing taller greatest

3 When a vowel is followed by *l* at the end of words, double the *l* before adding *er ed ing*:
   travel/*traveller* – *travelling* cancel/*cancelled*
   signal/*signalled*
   Exceptions: parallel/*paralleled*

Silent Letters

These letters can occur at the beginning, middle or end of a word and are not spoken when pronouncing the word.

b	plum*b* lam*b* tom*b* dou*b*t	**k**	*k*nock *k*now *k*night
c	s*c*ythe s*c*issors	**l**	ta*l*k yo*l*k fo*l*k
ch	ya*ch*t	**m**	*m*nemonics (see page 31)
d	bri*d*ge we*d*ge he*d*ge	**n**	hym*n* autum*n* colum*n*
g	si*g*n (but not in signal)	**p**	*p*neumonia *p*salm recei*p*t
	*g*nash *g*nat *g*naw	**t**	lis*t*en glis*t*en whis*t*le
gh	bri*gh*t hi*gh* bou*gh*	**u**	bisc*u*it g*u*ard
	throu*gh* ei*gh*t	**w**	*w*rite *w*rist *w*reck
h	*h*eir *h*our		

ph pronounced f
photograph   telegraph   telephone   elephant   physical
orphan

gh pronounced f
cough   trough   rough   laugh   draught

gh pronounced g
ghost   ghastly   gherkin   ghetto   ghoul   aghast

𝖂ords with a *q*

In the English language, *q* is almost always followed by *u*:
    queue   quick   conquer   plaque
(Some proper nouns, for example place names, may disobey this rule eg *Qatar*).

DO NOT CONFUSE SOME RELATED NOUNS AND VERBS

noun	*verb*
advice	to advise
practice	to practise
licence	to license

eg *The man was grateful for the good **advice**.*   NOUN
*She **practised** the song every day.*   VERB

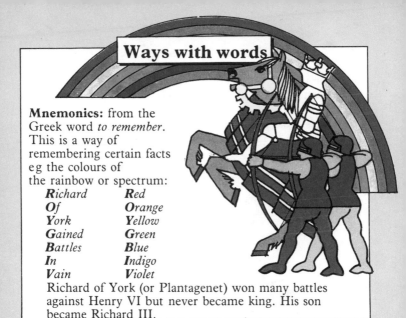

Ways with words

Mnemonics: from the Greek word *to remember*. This is a way of remembering certain facts eg the colours of the rainbow or spectrum:

Richard	**R**ed
Of	**O**range
York	**Y**ellow
Gained	**G**reen
Battles	**B**lue
In	**I**ndigo
Vain	**V**iolet

Richard of York (or Plantagenet) won many battles against Henry VI but never became king. His son became Richard III.

Palindrome: from the Greek meaning *to race again*. It is a word, phrase or sentence which reads the same backwards as forwards:

> *level   madam   deed*
> *Was it a cat I saw?*
> *Able was I ere I saw Elba.* (This relates to Napoleon's exile on the island of Elba.)

Some dates are also the same in reverse as forwards:

> *28.7.82   19.2.91*

Anagram: an anagram is the re-arrangement of letters in a word to make a new word or phrase. It is frequently used in crossword puzzles:

> eg *a rat's nest...neat stars*

Acronyms: an acronym is a word formed from the initial letters of other words:

> OPEC   UNESCO   AWOL   NAAFI
> NATO   NALGO

See end papers for definitions.

Prefixes and suffixes

The meaning of a word can be changed by adding letters to the beginning or end of the main word. **Pre** means *before* and **suff** means *after*.

Both words come from the Latin for **before** and **after**.

PREFIXES			MEANINGS	EXAMPLES
a			on as in	afloat aboard
a	*ab*	*abs*	from away	absent averse
ad	*ac*	*ar*	to	accept arrival advise
ante			before	ante meridiem *(am before noon or morning)*
bi	*bis*		two or twice	biennial bicycle biscuit *(cooked twice)*
circum			around	circumspect circumference
com			with together	companion communicate
contra			against	contradict contrary
de			down	detract deter demote
dis	*dif*		not	distaste differ
ex			out of	exit exhale expire
fore			before	foreword forecast
im	*in*		into	import include

PREFIXES	MEANINGS	EXAMPLES
in *im*	not	impossible immune incapable
inter	between	interval interrupt
mis	wrong	mistake misapply
ob	against	obstruct object
post	after	postpone postwar
pre	before	prefix preface prepare
pro	for forth	propose profit produce
re	back again	repeat remain retake
sub	under below	substandard submarine submerge
trans	across	transport transfer translate
un	not	unusual uninhabited undetected
vice	deputy instead of	vice chairman vice captain

SUFFIXES	MEANINGS	EXAMPLES
-able *-ible*	capable of	suitable edible
-ain *-an*	connected to	publican chaplain
-ance *-ence* *-ment* *-ness*	in a state of	repentance existence amusement hopelessness
-ant *-er* *-eer* *-ier*	someone who	servant assistant grocer engineer
-ess	female form	lioness princess
-fy	to make	magnify purify
-less	without	timeless fearless
-ling *-ock*	little	duckling bullock
-ory	a place for	factory
-ous	full of	monstrous victorious

33

Punctuation Marks

A full stop is used at the end of a sentence.

- It is becoming more common to omit full stops for initials and abbreviations:

    A.A. or *AA* *B.B.C.* or *BBC*
    department/*dept* Limited/*Ltd*

, A comma is used to separate phrases in a sentence, or when a list is being written. When reading aloud, pause at a comma.

John, bring me some groceries please.

; A semi-colon is a full stop above a comma. It is used to join two sentences instead of a conjunction.

Mind that paint; it is wet.

: A colon is used before a list.

Many people came: painters, architects, draughtsmen and engineers.

! An exclamation mark is used after interjections which indicate surprise, amazement, shock or delight, or at the end of a sentence.

Oh! Ah! Goodness! Help!
What a lovely surprise!

"What a lovely surprise!"

? A question mark is used at the end of a sentence, instead of a full stop, when something is being asked.

>*What are you doing?*

" " Inverted commas are used to indicate the exact words which are being said.

>*"Do you want to play with my toys?" Deborah asked Graham.*
>(See direct and reported speech section, page 36)

- A hyphen is used to join two or more short words:

>*jack-in-the-box*

or between syllables of one word split between two lines of writing. Try to avoid this wherever possible.

"What are you doing?"

( ) Brackets are used around additional words which are not essential to the main part of the sentence but which add more information:

>*John Bunyan wrote part of* Pilgrim's Progress *(published 1678) in prison.*

★ An asterisk is sometimes used to draw your attention to a note giving more facts at the bottom of a page.

35

Direct Speech

Watch out, James! You are too close to that tree.

" " OR ' ' are inverted commas also known as quotation marks or speech marks.

The actual words spoken are put inside the inverted commas – there are several ways to write the following:

a   *Brian said, "Watch out, James! You are too close to that tree."*

b   *"Watch out, James!" Brian said. "You are too close to that tree."*

   "Watch out, James! You are too close to that tree," said Brian.

Everything **inside** the bubble goes **inside** the inverted commas.

Question marks and exclamation marks also go inside the inverted commas, because they are a part of the sentence being quoted.

> *James asked, "What shall I do now? My line is tight."*

When the person speaking says more than one sentence, the inverted commas are not closed until the very end, and in line *b* Brian said is put in between the spoken words.
To show this the inverted commas are used after *James* and before *you*.

To avoid repetition of the word *said* and *ask*, try to use a variety of similar words which indicate speech:

> *exclaim   reply   answer   shout   tell   demand*
> *enquire   explain*

Reported Speech

No inverted commas are needed for reported speech because the exact words spoken are not used.

> Brian told James to watch out because he was too close to the tree. James wanted to know what to do when his line was tight.

Reported speech is used in newspaper articles, TV news broadcasts and when someone is telling another person about an event which has already happened.

Derivations

Many of our words have their origins in the Greek, Latin and French languages. Some have been taken from such sources as Russian, German, Indian and American Indian words. New words are still being made and used, particularly in science and technology, and these are derived from Latin and Greek.

Greek Origins

ENGLISH	GREEK	ORIGINAL MEANING	SOME PRESENT DAY MEANINGS
biology	*bios*	life, living organisms	the study of living things, their structure etc
	logos	speech or reason	
technology	*techne*	art, skill	practical or mechanical sciences
	logos	speech or reason	
calligraphy	*kallos*	beauty	beautiful writing, as an art form
chaos	*khaos*	time before the universe was ordered	utter confusion and disorder
palindrome	*palin*	again	a word or phrase which reads the same backwards and forwards – e g ewe
	dromos	course or race	
pseudonym	*pseudo*	false	false, pretending, a fictitious name
	nym	name	
telephone	*tele*	far	an instrument for relaying the sound of a voice over long distances
	phone	sound, voice	

Latin Origins

ENGLISH	LATIN	ORIGINAL MEANING	SOME PRESENT DAY MEANINGS
audience	*audire*	to hear, listen to	a group of listeners
agenda	*agere*	to do, act, set in motion	things to be done
capture	*capere*	to take, seize, take prisoner	to take someone prisoner, seize a place
captain	*caput*	head	the leader, someone in charge of team etc
dictionary	*dicere*	to speak, say, tell	a reference book of words, arranged alphabetically, to give meanings, pronunciations etc
decimal	*decem*	ten	number system based on tens
educate	*educare*	to lead out or draw out	to teach, instruct
fraction	*frangere*	to break, shatter,	a part of a whole
fracture		dash to pieces	a break (bone) a split (rocks etc)
interrogate	*rogare*	to ask	to closely question
lavatory	*lavare*	to wash	a toilet, WC
sinister	*sinister*	left (Romans thought the left suspect, not normal)	evil, treacherous
dexterous	*dexter*	right (normal)	someone good with their hands
script	*scribere*	to write	a written or printed text

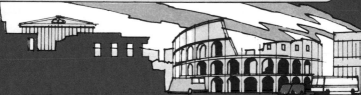

ENGLISH	LATIN	ORIGINAL MEANING	SOME PRESENT DAY MEANINGS
nature	*nascor*	to be born	animal and plant life,
natural	*nasci*		not artificial,
nativity	*natus*		original tribe, person
native			born in certain place
transport	*trans*	across	to move something
	portare	to carry	from one place to another
translucent	*lucere*	to shine	allows light to shine through
video	*videre*	to see	visual record

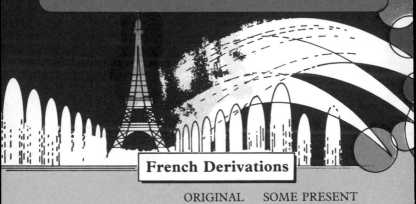

French Derivations

ENGLISH	FRENCH	ORIGINAL MEANING	SOME PRESENT DAY MEANINGS
chef	*le chef*	the chief, leader	principal cook in a restaurant
café	*le café*	qahwah – Arabic for coffee	a small inexpensive restaurant
journal	*journée*	a day	a daily record book, periodical
in lieu		in place	instead of
rendez-vous	*rendre*	to meet	a meeting place

Miscellaneous Derivations

ENGLISH	SOURCE	ORIGINAL MEANING	SOME PRESENT DAY MEANINGS
assassin	Arabic *hashshashin*	one who takes hashish	a murderer, especially political killings
geyser	old Norse *geysa*	to gush	a hot water spring
ghoul	Arabic *ghul*	he seized	an evil spirit, grave robber
bungalow	Hindi *bangla*	house	a one-storey house
gymkhana	Hindi *gendkhana*	ball house	a horse riding event
khaki	Urdu *khak*	dust	dull coloured cloth for army uniform

Derivations from People's Names

Tradescantia	*John Tradescant 1608-1662*	English botanist	plant family or a house plant
Fuchsia (say *few-sha*)	*Leonard Fuchs 1501-66*	German botanist	flowering plant from N. America
spoonerisms	*W A Spooner 1844-1930*	English clergyman	mixing up initial letters eg *a flied pie catcher* for *a pied fly-catcher*
wellingtons	*Duke of Wellington defeated Napoleon 1815*	he wore black leather knee high boots	water proof boots
cardigan	*Earl of Cardigan*	fought in Crimean War	a knitted button-up jacket

17 Mayfield Avenue
Fairfield Green
Washford
Cumbria
TNO 6AH

Letter Writing

Letters should contain certain pieces of information in the correct order:

1 the full address of the sender, including the postcode in the UK
2 the date written
3 the receiver's name
4 the information
5 the correct ending
6 the sender's name *

Women who do not wish to indicate whether or not they are married use Ms instead of Miss or Mrs.

The way you begin and end a letter depends on who is to receive it:

To someone you DO NOT KNOW: to a business group to a group of unknown people	Dear Sir, Dear Madam, Dear Sir or Madam,
and end	Yours truly or Yours faithfully plus your signature
to someone whose name you know but is not a close friend	Dear Mr and Mrs Roe,
and end	Yours truly or Yours sincerely plus your signature

Yours faithfully
Leslie Blake

to a close friend or friends

Dear Jim and Kathy

and end

Yours affectionately or
Yours ever or
Your old friend
plus your first name

to a relative

Dear Mum

and end

Love from.
plus your name

Postcards

People use postcards for messages which are short and are not private. The sender's address is not needed.

Dear John
    Everything arranged
for weekend.
    Leave Sunday 4p.m.
Hope to see all the family.

        Love Isabel

John Rushbrook
Moor Cottage
Crossways
BUDE
Cornwall
E2H 466

If a plain postcard is used, put the message on the blank side and the address in the space provided. Leave room for a stamp!

To Royalty

Letters to Royalty should be addressed to their Private Secretaries.

Start letter	*Address envelope*
Your Royal Highness	His/Her Royal Highness
to Royal Princes/Princesses	The Prince/Princess of...
or Royal Dukes/Duchesses	or the Duke/Duchess of...

To the Prime Minister

Dear Prime Minister	The Rt. Hon (Name) M.P.

To the Clergy

Church of England

Archbishops:	Dear Archbishop	The Most Rev and Rt Hon the Lord Archbishop of...
Bishops:	Dear Bishop	The Right Reverend the Lord Bishop of...
Vicars & Rectors	Dear Mr	The Reverend John or The Rev John and Mrs if wife included

Roman Catholic Church

The Pope:	Your Holiness Most Holy Father	His Holiness the Pope
Cardinals:	My Lord Cardinal	His Eminence the Cardinal Archbishop of...
	Your Eminence	His Eminence Cardinal if not Archbishop
Archbishops:	Dear Archbishop Your Grace	His Grace the Archbishop of...

Bishops:	My Lord Bishop	The Right Reverend
	Dear Bishop	John... Bishop of ...
Monsignors:	Dear Monsignor	The Reverend Monsignor
Priests:	Dear Father	The Reverend John

Addressing Envelopes

Leave sufficient room at the top right for the stamp. Try to balance the address so that it is not too cramped, nor too spaced out. Punctuation may be omitted and the lines may be staggered or level as in *a* or *b* below.

a
Mr and Mrs P Barman
35 Northfield Ave
Buckfastleigh
Devon
DE9 6HB

b
Mr and Mrs P Barman
35 Northfield Ave
Buckfastleigh
Devon
DE9 6HB

Words and Phrases

Synonyms: words with a *similar meaning*.

accuse	blame	rapid	quick	elude	escape
abandon	leave	regret	sorrow	courage	bravery
acute	sharp	coarse	rough	disaster	calamity
stern	strict	dusk	twilight	odour	smell

Antonyms: from the Greek word meaning *opposite name*.

Adjectives

cheap	expensive
difficult	easy
false	true
negative	positive
opaque	transparent
deep	shallow

Nouns

birth	death
war	peace
heads	tails
noise	silence
retreat	advance
famine	abundance

Verbs

to love	to hate
to ask	to tell
to shout	to whisper
to find	to lose
to deny	to admit
to buy	to sell

Cheap

20p

Expensive

£5

Birth

M.A LoVes T.D

Love

Hate

DAILY NEWS

BRUTAL MURDER

Death

Homonyms: from the Greek word meaning *similar name*. These are words which sound or look alike but have different meanings.

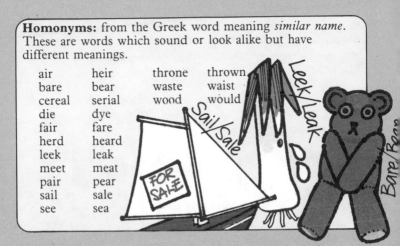

air	heir	throne	thrown
bare	bear	waste	waist
cereal	serial	wood	would
die	dye		
fair	fare		
herd	heard		
leek	leak		
meet	meat		
pair	pear		
sail	sale		
see	sea		

Proverbs: a proverb is a short, easily remembered phrase about an everyday fact:

Many hands make light work...
   a job is done more quickly if everyone helps.
The early bird catches the worm...
   be early if you want something special.
Birds of a feather flock together...
   people with similar interests get on well.
Half a loaf is better than none...
   be grateful for anything you get.

Similes: from the Latin word meaning *like*.

   as black as coal or soot
   as cool as a cucumber
   as quick as lightning
   as slippery as an eel
   as wise as an owl
   as poor as a churchmouse
   as slow as a snail

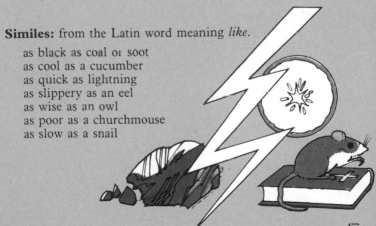

Metaphors: from the Greek word meaning *to transfer*.

A metaphor compares two things without using the words like or as:

> *He was a lion in battle.*

The characteristics of the lion are transferred to the man.

The *metaphor* would become a *simile* if we used *like* or *as*:

> *He was as brave as a lion in battle.*

'A chip off the old block'

Colloquialisms: from the Latin word for *conversation*: a colloquialism is a colourful phrase, used in conversation.

> *a chip off the old block*...describes a child who is very like a parent.
>
> *a rough diamond*...is someone who may have rough manners but has good intentions.
>
> *a wet blanket*...is someone who dampens other people's enthusiasm.

Colour Associations: Colours are often used in speech to help to describe a meaning:

eg *Red*

> *a red herring*...is not a fish but a false clue to lead someone off the scent.
>
> *to see red*...is to be very angry.
>
> *to be in the red*...is to spend more money than you have.
>
> *a red letter day*...is a very special day.

Other colours are used too.

> *green-eyed monster*...jealousy
>
> *he's yellow*...he's a coward
>
> *blue blood*...belonging to an aristocratic family
>
> *black sheep of the family*...a disgrace to the family
>
> *a white elephant*...something of little value

Surname Derivations

The origins of some of our surnames are obvious e g Archer, Carpenter. Others are more obscure because they may have changed considerably since they were first used. Surnames or family names are not like first or given names. The surname grew out of the need to distinguish one John from another: *John the cook* or *John the barber*. Where he lived may have been the way to identify him: *John on the hill* or *by the brook*. He may have had a very distinctive appearance such as *John the wild*, *John the longfellow* or *John the whitehead*.

It is thought that by the reign of Richard II (1377-1399) surnames were fixed and no longer referred to the persons bearing them.

Here are some interesting examples.

Occupations
Cooper...*made barrels*
Cutler...*made knives*
Fletcher...*made arrows*
Smith...*made things from metal*
Turner...*made small wooden bowls*

Home or Place of Birth
Fleming *(from Flanders)*
Hawthorne
Sykes *(very small stream)*
Thorp(e) *(small village)*
Greenwood

Appearance or Character
Jolly
Spenlow *(spend love)*
Shakespeare
Armstrong

Others
Elsie...*elf warrior*
Darwin...*dear friend*
Edward...*rich guard*
Godwin...*good friend*

The Calendar

DAYS OF THE WEEK: 7

Sunday means Sun's day. People once worshipped the sun as a god because of its importance to agriculture. The Romans named Sunday.

Monday means Moon's day. The Anglo-Saxons named a day after the moon to please it.

Tuesday Tiw was the Anglo-Saxon god of war.

Wednesday Woden's day. Woden was Tiw's father. The Anglo-Saxons believed that Woden made the world.

Thursday Thor or Thunor was the god of thunder. It was believed that thunder was the sound of Thor's chariot racing across the sky.

Friday Frigg was Woden's wife and the goddess of love and marriage.

Saturday Saturn was the Roman god of farming.

Anglo Saxon treasures, including a buckle with a representation of their god Woden.

MONTHS OF THE YEAR: 12

January Janus was the Roman god with two faces, one facing forwards, one backwards. He was the doorkeeper of the year.

February Februare in Latin means to purify. The Romans had a period of religious purification similar to Lent.

March This was originally the first month of the year named after Mars, the Roman god of war.

April The meaning is uncertain but it may be from the Latin word aperio which means I open and may refer to buds and flowers.

May There are two theories: one that May is named after Maia, the Roman goddess, the mother of Mercury; or after Maiores, the senior branch of the Roman government.

June From the Latin Junius, a Roman aristocratic family to which Brutus, one of Caesar's assassins, belonged.

July This month was originally named Quintilis and was the fifth month of the year. It was renamed in honour of Julius Caesar.

August was originally Sextilis (6th month). It was renamed after Augustus Caesar, nephew and heir of Julius.

September was originally the seventh month before July and August were added. Septem is Latin for seven.

October was the eighth month before the alteration. Octem is Latin for eight.

November was the ninth month...novem is Latin for nine.

December was the tenth month...decem is Latin for ten.

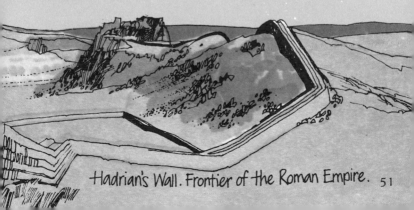

Hadrian's Wall. Frontier of the Roman Empire.

NCO non-commissioned officer

NEC National Exhibition Centre

NF National Front

NFU National Farmers' Union

NFWI National Federation of Women's Institutes

NSB National Savings Bank

NT National Trust

NUGMW National Union of General and Municipal Workers

NUM National Union of Mineworkers

NUS National Union of Seamen; Students

NUT National Union of Teachers

OBE Order of the British Empire

OHMS On His/Her Majesty's Service

OPEC Organisation of Petroleum Exporting Countries

OU Open University; Oxford University

PA personal assistant; publicity agent; Press Association

PAYE pay as you earn (income tax)

P&L profit and loss

P&O Peninsular and Orient (shipping line)

PC Police Constable; Parish Council; post card

PDSA People's Dispensary for Sick Animals

PE Physical Education

PhD or **DPhil** Doctor of Philosophy

PLO Palestinian Liberation Organisation

PO Post Office; Petty Officer; Personnel Officer; Pilot Officer

PTA Parent Teacher Association

PTO Please turn over

PS Police Sergeant; Private Secretary; post script

QC/KC Queen's/King's Counsel

QED Quod erat demonstrandum (which was to be shown)

RAC Royal Automobile Club

RADA Royal Academy of Dramatic Art

RAF Royal Air Force

RC Roman Catholic

RE Religious Education; Royal Engineers

RUFC Rugby Union football club

RIP Rest in peace

RN Royal Navy

RNLI Royal National Lifeboat Institution

ROSPA Royal Society for the Prevention of Accidents

RSPB Royal Society for the Protection of Birds

RSPCA Royal Society for the Prevention of Cruelty to Animals

RSVP Répondez-s'il vous plait. French for please reply to an invitation

SAYE Save as you earn (in the post office)

SLR Single lens reflex (camera)

SPCK Society for Promoting Christian Knowledge

STD Subscriber trunk dialling (telephone)

TGWU Transport & General Workers' Union

TNT trinitrotoluene – explosive

TUC Trades Union Congress

UAR United Arab Republic

UDI Unilateral Declaration of Independence (a breakaway from parent state)

UDR Ulster Defence Regiment

UFO unidentified flying object

UHF ultra high frequency

UK United Kingdom (England, Scotland, Wales & N. Ireland)

UN United Nations

UNESCO United Nations Educational, Scientific & Cultural Organisation

UNICEF United Nations Children's Fund

UNO United Nations Organisation

USA United States of America

USSR Union of Soviet Socialist Republics

VAT value added tax